By Bruno Hächler

PABLO
THE PIG

Illustrated by Nina Spranger

Translated by J. Alison James

A Michael Neugebauer Book

North-South Books

New York/London

The first rays of sun crawled over the roof of Pablo's hut. Pablo grunted, snorted, and blinked his eyes. Then he yawned deeply and snuggled back into the warm straw. The air was still cool, so he decided to sleep for another hour. Or two.

Pablo lived in a field at the edge of the town. People said that houses were going to be built there someday, but that didn't bother Pablo. Actually, nothing seemed to bother Pablo. He was completely content just rooting around for tasty plants and lolling in the mud until he was a luscious shade of brown. Pablo was a practical pig.

When he was little, Pablo had been a performer in a show. Every evening he rode across the stage in a baby carriage. When the audience saw his rosy little face, they laughed and clapped. That made Pablo happy.

Pablo grew and grew. Soon his head and curly tail rose above the edge of the carriage. People in the audience laughed even more. Pablo was still happy.

Pablo kept growing. Then one day he had grown so big that right in the middle of a performance the carriage crumpled beneath him.

The audience laughed louder than ever, but the laughter wasn't nice at all.

Pablo was humiliated. He ran squealing off the stage. Never again would he sit in a baby carriage.

That was when he came to the meadow. His friends from the show built him a little hut. They came to see him from time to time, bringing him delicious food—dry bread, salad, corncobs, and potatoes. Best of all were the apples. When Pablo bit into the sweet fruit and the juice dripped on his tongue, he squealed with glee.

Pablo's best friend was Vera. He loved it when she stroked his ears and scratched the bristles on his back. Vera told him stories. And sometimes she told him a secret. He could be trusted with secrets.

When Pablo was in high spirits, he nudged Vera with his snout and made her do a somersault.

"Hey, don't be so pushy!" she scolded. But she was giggling.

One day when Vera came to visit Pablo, she saw a dreadful sight—
Pablo's little hut was gone! A giant digger loomed like a yellow monster,
its teeth glinting dangerously. Vera knew what that meant. Soon
workers would come and start building houses. Pablo would have
to go.

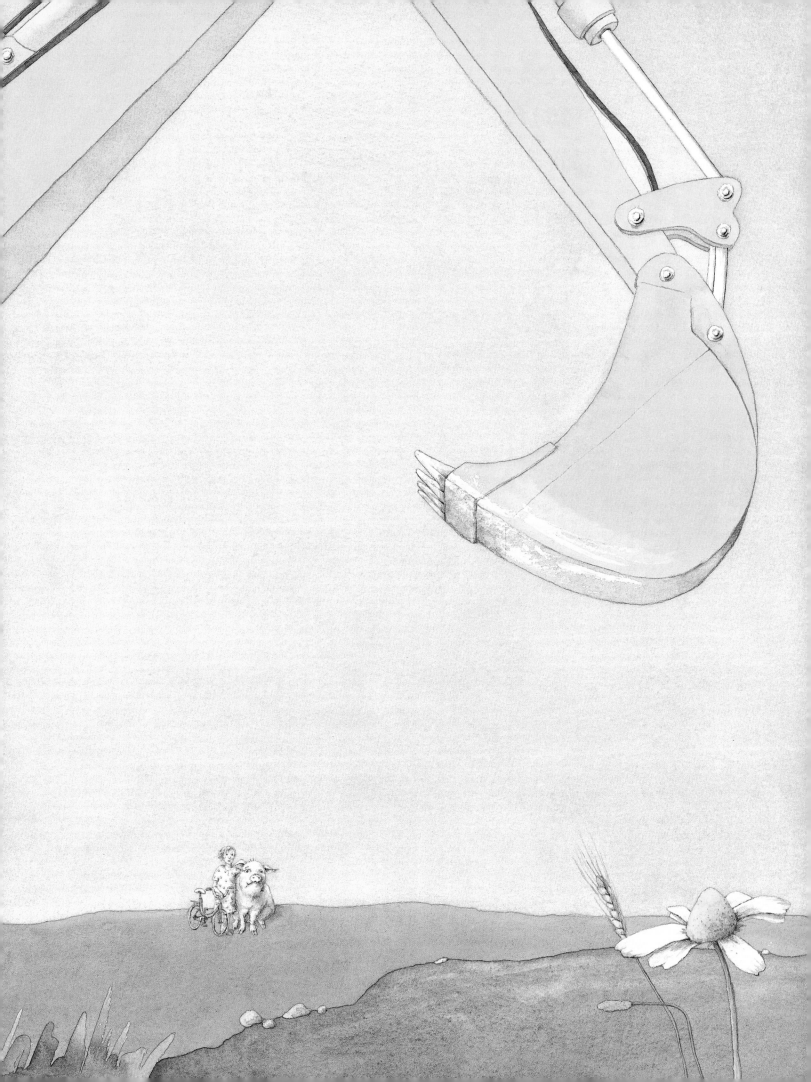

Vera dropped her bike in the grass and ran to hug Pablo. She was scared. In her school she'd seen pictures of pigs in captivity. There were no juicy roots, no sunshine, no mud. She imagined how sad Pablo would be in a cage. Who would talk to him? Scratch his back? Who would bring him his apples?

Then Vera heard the rumble of a motor and the screech of brakes.

Two men drove up in a butcher's van. They were heading
straight for Pablo!
"Run, Pablo! Run away!" Vera cried.
In a panic, Pablo leaped up and ran. He shot like a cannonball,
out of the meadow and into the town.

Pablo ran so fast his curly tail stuck out straight.
He ran and ran and ran.

Pablo didn't stop until he came to a sweet-smelling garden.
Carefully, he squeezed through the half-open gate.

The garden belonged to Mrs. Swift. She couldn't believe her eyes when, suddenly, an enormous pig hurried past her and tried to hide in her blackberry bushes. Then, right on his heels, raced a little girl who crouched beside the pig defiantly.
The woman put her hands on her hips. "Just what are you two doing?" she asked.

Vera's heart was pounding. Haltingly, she told the woman about Pablo.

Mrs. Swift listened in silence. Vera wiped the tears from her cheeks and stroked Pablo's ears lovingly. The woman studied the girl and the pig for a long time.

At last she smiled. "If you promise to take care of him, Pablo can stay here with me."
Now Vera's heart pounded with joy. She hugged Pablo, and Pablo squealed gleefully.

Then the two butchers arrived, grumbling and scolding. They wanted that pig! But when Mrs. Swift showed them Pablo lying happily in her garden, with Vera beaming beside him, the men gave up with a laugh. Empty-handed, they tramped away.

Pablo felt right at home in his new garden. Every morning and every evening, Vera came to visit him. His other friends came, too. They brought him dry bread, salad, corncobs, and potatoes. Best of all, right there in the garden was a great old tree that softly dropped sweet apples on the ground. Pablo ate his fill, grunting and sighing happily. He was a completely contented pig once more.

Copyright © 2002 by Michael Neugebauer Verlag, an imprint
of Nord-Süd Verlag AG, Gossau Zürich, Switzerland.
First published in Switzerland under the title *Pablo*.
English translation copyright © 2002 by
North-South Books Inc., New York.

First published in the United States, Great Britain, Canada,
Australia, and New Zealand in 2002 by North-South Books,
an imprint of Nord-Süd Verlag AG, Gossau Zürich, Switzerland.

Distributed in the United States by North-South Books Inc., New York.

Library of Congress Cataloging-in-Publication Data is available.
A CIP catalogue record for this book is available from The British Library.
ISBN 0-7358-1566-6 (trade edition)
1 3 5 7 9 HC 10 8 6 4 2
ISBN 0-7358-1567-4 (library edition)
1 3 5 7 9 LE 10 8 6 4 2
Printed in Italy

For more information about our books, and the authors and artists
who create them, visit our web site: www.northsouth.com